Mrs. Roskowski

Clifford's
Halloween

Norman Bridwell

SCHOLASTIC INC.

New York   Toronto   London   Auckland
Sydney   Mexico City   New Delhi   Hong Kong

To the real Emily Elizabeth's real friends:

Alison and Andrew

Melissa

Carolyn

Christian

Kate

and Mrs. Gallagher

ISBN 978-0-545-21595-4

Library of Congress Cataloging-in-Publication Data is available.

12 11 10 9 8 7 6 5 4 3 2 1   11 12 13 14 15

Printed in the U.S.A.   40
This edition first printing, July 2011

I'm Emily Elizabeth.
Today is a holiday! It's my
favorite day of the year.

This is my dog, Clifford.
Today is his favorite day, too.

With a big red dog like Clifford, every day is fun.
But holidays are the most fun of all.

At Christmas, Clifford makes a very good Santa.
He already has a red coat.

And on New Year's Eve, we stay up until midnight so
Clifford can blow his New Year's horn—

Happy New Year!

On Valentine's Day—

—Clifford is my favorite valentine.

And you should see Clifford on Easter.
He makes a wonderful Easter bunny.

On April Fool's Day,

Clifford never plays tricks on anyone . . .

and no one plays tricks on Clifford.

On Thanksgiving, Clifford gets a great big turkey.

But today is the best holiday of all—

HALLOWEEN!

Last year we had a big Halloween party.
I dressed as a pirate, but I didn't know
how to dress Clifford.

Daddy thought Clifford would make a good devil.

I wanted him to be a clown . . .

or maybe a witch.

But Clifford wanted to be—

a ghost.

When the children came to the party, nobody could guess who the big ghost really was.

We had fun.
We bobbed for apples.

Clifford wanted to play, too.

We played another game with apples.

Clifford won that game.

Then Mommy told us a ghost story.
But we weren't afraid . . .

We had the biggest ghost on our street taking care of us.

After the party, Clifford and I went trick-or-treating.

We didn't have much luck.
But we didn't mind.

It was time to go to bed anyhow.
Halloween was over.

And now Halloween has come again.

I am not going to be a pirate this year.

I am going to be a fairy princess.

But what should Clifford be?

An Indian chief?

A knight?

What do you suggest?